WHIP 2

Whip's Christmas Adventure

The Second Whip Book by

Tyler Johns

 www.trafford.com
North America & international
toll-free: 1 888 232 4444 (USA & Canada)
fax: 812 355 4082

CONTENTS

Okay! You want to know the new characters in this book? Alright I'll tell you. On the title page you see Whip in the middle, and on the right are Bobi (the crocodile) and Pition (the snake). On the left are two white tigers while on the bottom right is a walrus.

Abmora Satvrinski-the Tsarina of Siberia; she is a powerful provider of the best education to every earthly creature. The mother of Prince Aborabor.

Aborabor (pronounced: uh-BOR'uh-bor) Satvrinski-the crown prince of the white tigers of Siberia.

Fentruck Tusker-An experimental full-grown walrus. He shall be a new friend to Whip.

Notice: You will not believe who would spring for a new and better psychiatrist than any other.

PROLOGUE

Remember Them?

Remember the story of the mythical creature, Whip Psy, and his two reptilian pals, Bobert "Bobi" Gatorson the crocodile and Pition Vipers the black python?

Well, here's something new for the Whip team. Tail kickers are coming to everything. Just wait until they have new members.

CHAPTER 1

The Coming of Prince Aborabor

"There once was a mythical creature never told before. It was known as the "psyvark". It lived somewhere in Virginia. You'll realize what education it has. With that and forcing powers, it will always conquer the world."

-Prince Aborabor Satvrinski reading a book

Now to the story, the crown prince of the white tigers read the new diction of the psyvark and decided to head for Virginia.

"It is he," he said, "who will find out anything about myths and legends throughout the world." Obeying his mother's word, Aborabor was told to take the quest to Virginia, to discover the untold myth.

To maneuver his voyage, he rode a ship from Spain after crossing the whole continent of Europe on a motorcycle for many days. He spoke to himself.

"Across the Atlantic Ocean," he said, "west to the east coast of the United States of America, the wisest dynasty of Earth shall secure the ignorant of one species."

He found the town of Psyville between Virginia and West Virginia. Then he found the home of the Psy family the next day, sneaking up on Tehran and Corbin Psy's daughter, Sarah's window on a ladder climbing the roof. In a stealthy way, he could tell what children like in their rooms, just as he recognized the perfect choice of a bedroom for a young female creature.

"It will be she," Aborabor said, "who will be chosen…" he walked through the window into Sarah's bedroom. "…for a real education besides—HOUGH!" He panicked as he noticed a dragon lying on the bed.

"What do you need?" asked the dragon.

"Is…Sarah…Psy here?" asked Aborabor.

"No, she's at school," said the dragon.

"Oh!" said Aborabor. "Well, who are *you* by the way?"

"Fredwick," the dragon answered. "I'm Sarah's stuffed toy dragon. I usually come to life when nobody's around except her."

"Ah, I see." Aborabor walked out the window and leaped off the roof onto his motorcycle. "I can't wait to tell my mother the truth," he said driving back to the east coast.

CHAPTER 2

Just Another Day of Chit-Chat

As our three main heroes, Whip, Bobi, and Pition seemed ready for winter during their senior year in high school, the chatted with their human lunch pal, Gavin.

"So how are your sophomore classes going so far, Gavin?" asked Whip.

"Man," said Gavin, "I flunked my geometry class, and now I have a different schedule."

"Any problems?" asked Pition.

"All these elementary school cartoons I remembered in those computer programs just reminded me of the lessons I learned in my classes from last year," said Gavin.

"Yeah," said Bobi, "life's just weird that way. We remember everything from our early schools."

So those boys ate their lunches.

CHAPTER 3

Eric the Psycho Kid

As the main guys ate their lunches, another human kid named, Eric, chatted with his friends.

"Hey, guys, check this out!" Eric called out. "It's that dorky creature with his scaly friends at that table over there!" Suddenly, he scooped a hunk of his Jell-O, and then readied it like a catapult by thumbing the blade of his spoon.

"Ready," he said, "aim...fire!" He flicked his spoon of Jell-O toward Whip and his friends.

As Whip saw the Jell-O, he asked out loud, "Who's responsible?!"

One of the kids by Eric pointed to Eric.

"That's the psycho kid who did it," he said.

Whip went toward that table. Bobi and Pition followed him.

"Are you guys nuts?!" Gavin called to them.

Eric got up from his eating place, putting his arms up folded in front of himself, with his fists clenched. Whip did the same thing. Eric put his arms down and laughed really hard for seconds. Whip came closer to him and gave him a giant punch in the face. Eric fell down crying in vain. Then he got up and said, "I'll get y-you f-for this!" Then he ran to the principal's office.

"Mission accomplished, guys," Whip said to his friends.

As they walked out of the cafeteria, a campus supervisor parked a golf car in front of the three friends. He had them come into the car as he took them to the office. And so, they were to have a lecture with the principal. Eric had explained what had happened during lunch. Then the principal sent him to the nurse's office.

"What have you boys got to say for yourselves?" asked the principal.

"Well, Mr. Yupnacht," Whip started to explain, "we kind of got off on the wrong foot when Eric shot his Jell-O at us."

"I think he needs a psychiatrist," said Pition. So the principal sent the three guys back to their classes.

CHAPTER 4

Elementary School Fights: Boys Against Girls

And so before we can get back to the heroes, I have to tell you this other story. On the Eastern Boundary Elementary School playground, the girls were having a long chat, all of the girls except for Sarah Psy, swinging on the swing in the bark pit.

As those girls chatted on the basketball court, the boys snuck up under fences. Bobi's twin kid brothers, Mobi and Maudi, stood in charge. They decided to go first. As they did Mobi secretly snuck up between some of the girls by slithering, then he suddenly sprang up and said, "Okay, everyone, listen up! Girl talk's over, so scram! The boys and I are gonna play basketball!"

"Okay," said a little female frog named, Amy Boo, "can *we* play with you guys?"

"No," said Mobi. "You suck. Why don't you run home and play with some of your stupid doll houses."

"Yeah," said a young male raccoon named, Quasimodo Fletcher, "or if you're still immature, go to a nursery or..."

"Stop acting sarcastic, you twerp!" said a fourth grade female rat named, Tammy Doxton.

"Hey, lighten up, Tammy!" shouted Maudi. "No one talks like that to my coon friend, Quasi!" He walked toward Quasimodo saying, "Are you alright, pal?"

"Yeah, I guess so," said Quasimodo.

The fight continued until a female bear cub named, Jessica Pawston, shouted out, "STOP! Everyone stop! As princess of this playground, I order you to quit fighting. Let us all have it shared."

"Well you're otherwise known as 'Princess Poop-face'," said Mobi. The children laughed.

"How rude!" Jessica frowned as she said that.

"We can't have your opinions now," said Quasimodo.

"Listen," said Mobi, walking toward Jessica. "We have a basketball game on Saturday, we've all had our permission slips signed, and there's only one good court to practice on…" he raised his scaly hands up to his chest, "…so make like a tree—and *beat it!*" He shoved Jessica. Then she fell to the ground. Mobi pinned her by the shoulders.

"You're gonna get detention for this!" Jessica yelled.

"Relax, we know CPR," said Mobi. "Come on, Maudi!" he called to his brother, heading towards him. "Give her some of your famous Beef Con Carne!"

"Con Carne! Con Carne! Con Carne!" the boys shouted. They repeated the word.

Suddenly, Maudi started to nearly sit on Jessica's face. He lifted his tail over his brother's head. Jessica panicked, closing her eyes. Maudi expanded a long fart.

Meanwhile, the other boys were putting up fights with the other girls. As for Quasimodo, to pay back for being called a "twerp", he tied up Tammy and gagged her with a "red flag" ribbon from the property closet by the restrooms.

Suddenly, the elementary school dean, Mr. Spurn, walked toward the children along with Pition's kid brother, Petro, slithering beside him, who told about the other children fighting. Just as the dean blew the whistle, Mobi and Maudi left Jessica, still lying on the asphalt ground.

"Later, 'Princess Poop-face'," they said, running off.

Mr. Spurn walked towards Jessica to check on her.

"Are you alright?" he asked.

"Yeah, I'm okay," Jessica said, waving the fart from her senses.

"Do we need to call your parents or something?" asked Mr. Spurn.

"No," said Jessica. "I'll get some fresh air myself." So she went off.

Mr. Spurn then found Tammy Doxton tied to a basketball pole. He untied the jump rope and the "red flag" ribbon over her mouth.

"Perhaps their manners with each other should have a few modifications," said Petro.

"They'll have to suffer however they play," said Mr. Spurn. So he decided to chat with the kids who had been fighting, blowing his whistle.

Meanwhile, back at Central Virginia High School, Whip and his friends waited for the bus to ride home.

"Did you guys get in trouble for Eric?" asked Gavin.

"Totally!" said Bobi.

"We got busted big fat time," said Pition.

Suddenly, a raccoon walked by. His name was Scoobert Fletcher.

"Hey, guys," he said.

"How's life, Scoobert?" asked Whip.

"Okay," said Scoobert. "My little brother, Quasimodo, is signed for a boys' basketball game this Saturday."

"So are *my* brothers," said Bobi.

"Hey, stooges!" called out a voice. It was the older guy named, Job, from what I talked about in the first book. "I heard you guys got in trouble today."

"Yeah," said Whip. "We're totally busted. Besides I've got to get home. Just need to wrap this talk up. I've got a letter to give to my parents." The buses arrived and the boys walked aboard.

CHAPTER 5

Sarah's Got a Problem

Meanwhile, back at the elementary school, Sarah was swinging on one of the swings in the bark pit. She swung faster and higher. Then at the highest height she jumped. Suddenly, as she fell to the bark, urine unexpectedly flowed out of her bladder, meaning she wet herself.

"Oh, great!" she complained. "Recess is over and I just completely wet myself." She thought about this for a second. "At least school's almost over. I guess I can keep my legs open the rest of the day."

As she went back to Mr. Grapestick's class (her teacher), she quickly grabbed toilet paper from a nearby restroom. Then she walked into class. While sitting at her desk, with toilet paper underneath her on her chair, she felt trauma running through her mind.

"Please let my teacher pick somebody else!" she panicked and worried. "I'll bet he has somebody special in mind."

"Sarah, will you do the next word problem?" Mr. Grapestick asked.

"Uh…I don't think so," said Sarah.

"What do you mean 'you don't think so'?" Mr. Grapestick asked her. "It's quite obvious."

"I think you're going to have to do better than that."

Sarah sighed. So much for wetting myself, she said in her head. Then she did it again. Urine flowed out once again automatically. As Mr. Grapestick realized it, he slapped his face in an uproar. He thought if Sarah had a disease in her bladder. So he sent her to the nurse's office.

"Who will do the next problem?" Mr. Grapestick asked again. Then he saw a paw up from a female skunk student. "Ah yes, Cruella Disney, since you've been enjoying the lesson, why don't you come up here?"

"Thank you, Mr. Grapestick," said Cruella, walking up to the white board.

"She's so smart at like everything," said Mobi.

"I'll bet she grows up to be a scientist," said Maudi.

Meanwhile, at the nurse's office, Sarah had to remain in the restroom on the toilet for her problem. Mr. Grapestick knew that she should use a bag of diapers. And so, as the elementary school nurse brought a big bag of urinal guards, she knocked on the door and Sarah grabbed the bag and changed into one of those guards. "The only thing I need to worry about is staying in my room for any troubles I make," she said to herself.

After she changed, the nurse tried to make contact with the Psy family.

"So you must be Sarah Psy?" she wondered.

Sarah nodded her head.

"Your parents are busy," said the nurse. "What is your brother's cell phone number?"

"Uh…" Sarah thought for a second. "132-9458."

The nurse called the number.

Whip was at home doing his homework. His cell phone rang and he answered it. "Hello," he said.

"This is the elementary school nurse calling and I'm looking for Whip Psy," the nurse called.

"This is him," said Whip.

"Your sister has lost control of her bladder," said the nurse, "so I got her a diaper bag."

"Alright," said Whip. "I'll get her." He walked out of the house and into the parking lane. He went into his traveling invention, the World Bug 3000. As he drove to pick up his sister from school, he had a thought saying, she must have a lack of toilet-training.

Just as elementary school was over, Mobi and Maudi were excited when Cruella Disney broke several math records.

"Boy, I sure love Cruella's talents," said Mobi.

"Yeah," said Maudi. "She's so sexy like even if she lays on something…"

"Bro!" Mobi exclaimed.

"I was just being honest and realistic," said Maudi.

Sarah was sitting on the sidewalk, waiting for her brother. Suddenly, Petro Vipers approached her.

"Heard you had a problem, Sarah," he said, hissing.

"Yeah," said Sarah. "I just want to be alone." So, she sat and waited.

And so, Whip arrived, landing the World Bug in the bus lane from midair. Sarah walked toward her brother waiting. As they flew home, Whip interrogated with his sister.

"How on Earth did you lose control of your bladder?" he asked.

"I swung on a swing too high," said Sarah.

"Well, so you've got diapers to wear through this whole lifetime of yours," said Whip.

"Of course," said Sarah. "I blew it."

Meanwhile, in a secret meeting place in Canada, Abmora had to talk with her son.

"So you haven't found Sarah Psy yet, huh?" she asked.

"No," said Aborabor. "I found her stuffed toy dragon on her bed."

"The Psys will be sorry when I confront them," said Abmora.

CHAPTER 6

The Trauma Drama

As they got home, Sarah went up to her room feeling doubtful.

"So your teacher didn't notice that you wet your underpants until you did it again?" asked Fredwick, her stuffed dragon.

"I didn't have much of a choice," said Sarah. "I grossed the whole class out."

"So that's why you're home kind of early," said Fredwick.

"Yeah," said Sarah. "So I've got diapers to wear."

"That's hard to believe."

A while later, it was dinner time. Whip's mother, Corbin had lasagna baking in the oven. Sarah walked into the kitchen.

"What's for dinner tonight, Mom?" she asked.

"Lasagna," said Corbin.

They must have taken a policy for my eating habits, Sarah thought.

Another while passed, the dinner table was set, grace was said and the family started eating.

"What's this fuzzy white stuff?" Sarah asked.

"Ricotta cheese," said Corbin.

"This *is* delicious," said Sarah. "I thought I imagined eating frog vomit for a diet."

"Sarah, that's disgusting!" said Whip.

The father, Tehran, rested his forehead on his hand and sighed.

Sarah continued, "I can't imagine having laxative remove sugar towards my heart."

"That does it!" shouted Tehran. "Bed!" He sent Sarah to her room.

"I think that was harsh, Teh," said Corbin, "'cause she'll get hungry. And at least she's eaten some of her lasagna."

"Sarah's got to learn some manners," said Tehran. "She won't starve to death or anything."

"When I had to pick her up from school," said Whip, "I heard that she lost control of her bladder."

"We heard that from the elementary school nurse," said Corbin.

"Oh," said Whip.

Meanwhile up in her bedroom, Sarah felt guilty for the troubles she had made all along.

"Man, I sure blew the whole day," she said. "Now Dad has sent me to my room for a gross talk at dinner."

"What did they have to say about your bladder problem?" asked Fredwick.

"They talked to my teacher about my health issue at recess," said Sarah, "and everything I had said about it."

"Uh huh," said Fredwick.

"So they went back to my school and got the rest of my homework. Want to help me?"

"You're lucky dragons are so smart at all kinds of stuff."

So they did the homework together.

A while passed since Sarah was to stay in her room, and then it was her bedtime. She called out to her brother, "Whip! I want a bedtime story!"

"Go to bed, Sarah!" Whip called back. "I'm way too busy tonight! I'll read you one tomorrow or whenever!" He was working on his homework.

"If you don't read me a story," Sarah said, "I *won't* go to bed!"

"Ooh...someday..." Whip growled. So he walked up to his sister's room. He then looked around the shelves for a story.

"What story would you like tonight?" Whip asked.

"How about that one?" Sarah pointed to the book, entitled "Happy Endings".

"No, I don't want to read that again," said Whip. "Here's William Shakespeare's *A Midsummer Night's Dream*. You might like this story."

"Yeah," said Sarah. "How good can Shakespeare's stories be if some have good endings and some have bad endings?"

"That's because they're comedies and tragedies," said Whip. "They have stuff to do with drama."

"They're just boring," said Sarah.

"That's because most kids don't understand Shakespeare that easily. Do you want me to read to you or not? It's your choice."

"You're unbelievable. You're just acting like a stranger!"

"Oh yeah? Well, here's a news flash for you! Whether you like it or not, people can act like strangers all they want!" So Whip decided to leave the room. "I don't know why I let you talk me into this. Good night!" He turned off the light and closed the door.

"Well, what do you know about that?" said Fredwick. "Too much argument, no story."

"Go to sleep," said Sarah.

And so, the days went by. And that Saturday night the Eastern Boundary Elementary School boys played their basketball game against the boys from another elementary school in West Virginia. The Eastern Boundary Elementary School boys won.

After the game, Bobi drove his brothers home, and then they walked into their house.

"How was the game, boys?" asked Bobi's mother, Harley to Mobi and Maudi.

"We whizzed the other team," said Mobi. "We're geniuses," he said together with Maudi.

CHAPTER 7

Tehran Meets the Satvrinskis

And so, school was finally out for the winter of 2001. Then that night, Tehran stared out the window of his and his wife's bedroom, complaining about Sarah's moods, "I *knew* things would turn out this way. I can hardly believe *that*, Corbin, I mean really. She's the one with the problem, not *me.*"

"I think, Tehran, you're taking this far too seriously," said Corbin. "This is Sarah's decision on a subject."

"Well, yes, but she's supposed to choose one of the subjects here in the *real world,*" said Tehran. "I can't stand having any nonsense done by children. I mean you expect me to give my philosophy about this…this… trash of hers?!"

"Sarah does," said Corbin. "And she'll always be innocent of we do. I don't want to lose her to anyone, Teh."

"Ugh-hhh…humbug."

"Don't you remember back in college, you and me? We'd find our right species and we made out."

"Our mental health, our love, our reality, our children." Tehran began a rage of a tantrum. "It's not the same! I don't think you realize that our daughter has turned into a psychopath!"

"Ah-oh, stop being such a scrooge, Teh."

"Fine! Fine! Pretend nothing happened, blah wah wah wah blah!" Tehran sighed. "No one else can talk about that nonsense."

Suddenly, a helicopter lowered by the master bedroom's balcony.

"Tehran Psy," someone called from it.

Tehran jumped in distraction.

"What happened?" asked Corbin.

"Uh, nothing, dear, it's just the memories in my head," said Tehran. "I'm just stretching out here for a while." He closed the balcony doors.

The one calling his name was the tsarina, Abmora Satvrinski. "You better get in," she said as Tehran turned around. "We need to talk."

"Uh, actually, madam whoever you are," said Tehran, "I've just recently taken my sleeping pills and they're making me a bit drowsy…" a polarguard walked right behind him, herding him into the helicopter. "… so how about if we make this a quick one?" He walked all the way aboard as the guard walked on and closed the door. The helicopter lifted off.

"So…" said Tehran. "Who might you white tigers be?"

"My name is Abmora Satvrinski," said Abmora. "I am tsarina of Siberia, Russia. And this is my son, Prince Aborabor." She raised her paw in a horizontal position in front of her son.

"Abor…abor, ha ha, nice name," said Tehran. "Uh, when did you decide to drop by?"

"Oh, about two weeks ago actually," said Aborabor. "After a long trip across all of Europe, I rode my motorcycle to a harbor in Spain and rode a ship all the way here to America…"

"I'll handle the rest, son," Abmora interrupted, patting her son on the head. "So when he decided to drop by, he dropped into your daughter's room and found some ridiculous form of a dragon, telling him that your daughter was still at school that day."

"I mean it wasn't my fault," said Tehran. "You two were here slightly early."

"Of course we were," said Abmora. "So what do you have to say about that?"

"Well," said Tehran, "it seems that my daughter's imagination kept some poor education within her mind."

"Stop the helicopter!" Abmora shouted. The pilot slowly lowered on top of a building below. "Tehran," Abmora continued. "You have forced me to do something I really don't want to do." She opened the door.

"Augh!" Tehran panicked. "Where are we?"

A nearby public security office appeared in sight. "This building is not to be inhibited by terrorists; it is inconceivably inconveniencing," said a man from the security office.

"Another plan ruined!" yelled Abmora. "I hope you're happy." She frowned at Tehran. Then she turned to the officer. "I'm terribly sorry about all this. My men and I arrived in this nation for a certain reason. I am to help someone with wisdom."

"I'm writing your ticket," said the officer as he did. "You're fee is $250."

"You're lucky I'm very filthy rich," said Abmora, digging through one of her moneybags and paying the fee. So she grabbed the ticket and closed the helicopter door.

"Be careful next time," the security man said to the helicopter's pilot.

"As you wish," said the pilot, lifting off.

And so, the helicopter was to fly back to the Psy family's house to drop off Tehran.

"So," said Abmora, "your son *will* share his wisdom with your daughter."

"Yes," said Tehran.

"Oh, believe me, Tehran," said Abmora, flicking her security ticket, "it's what's best, not only for your family,…" she put her ticket into one of her gown's inside pockets. "…but for your species."

And so, they arrived back at the Psys' house, back by the balcony where Tehran was standing in the first place. Tehran walked off and jumped on the balcony.

"And what am I supposed to do about it?" he asked Abmora. Then she tossed one of her moneybags to him.

"Have a nice Christmas vacation," said Abmora. "You're meeting me in Canada." She closed the door and commanded the pilot to take off. Tehran went back to bed.

CHAPTER 8

Christmas Is Here

And so, fast-forwarding the story to Christmas morning, Whip was reading a book in bed while he was wide awake. Sarah was suddenly able to get up early.

"Fredwick, wake up," she said to her stuffed dragon, who was still sleeping. "It's Christmas."

"Are you sure?" asked Fredwick. "It's five in the morning."

"Let's see if Santa left out our goodies," said Sarah. She got out of bed along with Fredwick, and then they walked downstairs.

"I can hear the wind howl out the windows," said Fredwick.

As they got to the Christmas tree, Sarah checked the tags on each package, "This one's for Mom, this one's for Whip, this one's for Dad, Whip, Mom, Dad…Hey, where are *your* presents? Santa must have lost his marbles when I wrote your list of what you wanted."

"They're lucky that we, dragons, were the perfect gifts for children to begin with," said Fredwick.

"MOOOOOM! DAAAAAD!" Sarah called out. "SANTA DIDN'T BRING FREDWICK ANYTHING!"

"Another one of these days, our daughter wants an appeasement," said Corbin, waking up.

"It had better be a lot later than it feels like," said Tehran, hardly getting up.

Meanwhile, back by the tree, Sarah felt sorry about that if Santa Claus had ignored Fredwick's list. "Well here's a present from me, anyway," she said hugging Fredwick. "Hope it fits."

"Don't worry," said Fredwick. "The best gifts don't come in boxes. I'll treasure this one forever."

Meanwhile, the rest of the family walked to the tree.

"You always wake up out of bed earlier than the rest of us," Corbin said to Sarah. "Merry Christmas by the way, dear."

"I suppose the reason why Santa couldn't bring your dragon anything is because he's not real," said Tehran.

"Oh," said Sarah.

"Let's suppose he didn't know who 'Fredwick' was," said Whip.

"Yeah," said Sarah, "maybe you're right. I should've described him."

And so, the family opened their gifts. Whip opened a long package. Inside it was a skateboard.

"Ha," he said. "We'll say all ranges accepted in the sports alley."

Tehran brought a large washing machine for dishes from the kitchen into the living room, along with a wooden board with slits for sharp knives.

"Don't worry," he said. "We'll have lots of room for more dishes in this new one." He moved the dish washer and the knife board back to the kitchen.

Corbin looked at a present she received from her husband and said, "Teh, I thought I *had* a sweater that was brown and white like this."

"That's supposed to have more like a diamond-type design on it," said Tehran.

Sarah realized that she only received a few gifts from Santa. As she opened them, she said, "Santa must have taken out a policy on giving me a few presents, but not enough."

Well, hopefully the other presents should be good ones. Other kids around the town got coal for the fight at school. Mobi and Maudi got some, too.

CHAPTER 9

The Vacation Plan

Just as Christmas Day passed, Tehran commanded his family to pack up for the trip to Canada for winter vacation. Whip called his friends to ask them if they were interested. Whip called Bobi.

"Yes," said Bobi, "I'll pack and ask my mother."

Then Whip called Pition.

"Sure," said Pition. "Well, my cold blood often feels like liquid oxygen when I'm in the snow. But don't worry; I've got a warm slide-through suit for Christmas. It's a little snake thing." He grabbed that suit. "See you outside." He and Whip hung up.

"My friends are coming," said Whip.

"Alright, we'll make room," said Corbin.

The Psy family packed their stuff in a large white motor home that Tehran had rented from the Psyville Auto-mall. Just as Bobi and Pition went by the vehicle, Corbin had a terrible thought.

"I'm afraid the house can be torn down," she said.

"I've locked the front door," said Tehran. "No one will break in."

"Don't worry, we'll take care of everything," said a high, scratchy voice. It was Slippy the slug, one of the animals mentioned in the first book, which were under control of the Vips, until Whip and his friends found them. The animals opened a window and they shoved themselves in.

"Well, everything sums it," said Whip. He and his friends hopped aboard. Tehran started the motor home and they were off.

"Where are we going, Dad?" asked Sarah.

"Somewhere in Canada," said Tehran. "It will take about a day and a half."

"I can't wait to test my slide-through suit in the snow," said Pition.

The trip led them north, out of West Virginia, up through Maryland and stopped in Pittsburgh, Pennsylvania to find lunch.

"I sure feel tubby from that burger," said Sarah after they had McDonald's food for lunch.

"I sure feel lucky I won't have to eat like forever," said Pition, "'cause I've eaten a bunch of rats in my house two months ago."

At least Bobi was okay not to eat; he felt much like a predator after his family's Christmas dinner, eating a lot of turkey. Later they all left Pittsburgh.

"Can you tell me a story, Whip?" asked Sarah.

"Alright," said Whip, "here it goes." He began the story: "Once upon a time, there was an apple that had grown on a tree, until someone picked it and took a bite. Then that person threw it on the ground because of the sour taste of that green apple. Then…"

"Then ants started to finish it up for him, right?" Sarah asked as she interrupted the story.

"'Scuse me," said Whip, "who's telling this story? You or me?"

"Um…you," said Sarah.

"Exactly, so keep your mouth shut." Whip continued: "So the ants ate their fill and the apple rotted for many days until, guuurrrghhh!" He finished: "The end."

"Gross," said Sarah. "Lots of stories just touch my heart with cruelties."

"Oh, stop your malfunction and quit being such a baby," said Whip. *I swear her heart will start to rot if she doesn't take a bath*, he thought.

"I definitely knew we couldn't trust any children," said Pition to Bobi.

"Totally," they both said.

And so, they all reached Jamestown, New York.

"There's a restaurant up ahead," said Tehran, "want to stop?"

"Sure," said Corbin.

"Only if it's anything good," said Sarah.

"Sarah, we've fed you plenty of things you liked all your life," said Corbin.

"She knows I'm sick of this nonsense," said Tehran.

As the Psys stepped out of the motor home, Whip asked his friends, "Are you guys in the mood for food yet?"

"Nah, we're cool," said Bobi and Pition, so they waited.

So the Psy family feasted on steaks for dinner (just as they ordered). After dinner, the next planned stop was Buffalo.

"I have to go to the bathroom at number two," said Sarah.

"We just pulled out of that restaurant, Sarah," said Tehran. "We have a bathroom in the back to make you happy."

"Okay," said Sarah. So she walked to the motor home's bathroom. Bobi and Pition sat on the bed at the left side of the vehicle. Whip sat on one of the two chairs on the right side. The ride took everyone by Lake Erie. Then night came as they stopped by a hotel in Buffalo.

Next year, thought Tehran, I swear I'll just take a vacation by myself. So he paid the bill to check in.

CHAPTER 10

Someone Is Hiding in the Hotel

After Tehran checked into the Buffalo-Erie Hotel, the keeper gave him the key to room #214. So the Psys, Bobi, and Pition went to the central elevator tower. Tehran pressed the up button and the button to the second floor. The hotel had five floors. They searched the halls in a group until Whip found the room number on a nearby door. So they all went in. There were two beds, a television set on a long dresser, and one chair. Sarah jumped in the left bed feeling very sleepy. Whip slept next to her. Their parents took the right bed. Bobi and Pition decided to lay on the floor with their own blankets and pillows they had brought in the motor home.

"Man, I get the chills by snuggling with you," said Bobi to Pition.

"That's because we're reptiles," said Pition, "we're cold-blooded."

"Right," said Bobi.

All of a sudden, in the middle of the night, Tehran gained a thought from a forcing feeling. He got out of bed slowly, without waking anybody up. He opened the door and put the room key in his pocket; he put his glasses on. He walked to the central elevator tower and pressed the controls down to the first floor. He walked off the elevator, and then walked to the lobby. He talked to the kitchen bartender.

"Excuse me," he said. The bartender turned around from washing the dishes. Tehran interrogated, "I'm looking for somebody, taking care of a mysterious ruler."

"What sort of ruler?" asked the bartender.

"Well, it's like this," said Tehran, "a 'tsarina' wants to have my daughter learn better than she has in her school years."

"I see," said the bartender. "You know, there's only one fellow who can handle a job like that. He is a wise guy in a lot of places you can think of."

"Alright," said Tehran. "Where can I find him?"

"He's a walrus," said the bartender. "He's somewhere in this hotel's basement. Here's the room number." He handed Tehran a card that said #B24.

And so, following the bartender's instruction, Tehran walked back to the elevator. He pressed the down button and the elevator lowered down to the basement. He turned on surrounding lights in that underground hallway, looking for room #B24. Until at last, he found the door. He knocked on it, saying, "Room service!"

Suddenly, whoever was in there woke up and answered the door, opening it slowly.

"Hello," it was the walrus, the bartender told Tehran about. "May I help you?"

"Um, I beg your pardon," said Tehran. "My name is Tehran Psy and I was hoping if you're the one to talk about the white tiger tsarina, Abmora Satvrinski."

"You're told correct, sir," said the walrus. "My name is Fentruck Tusker."

"Pleasure," said Tehran. He dug into the money bag, which Abmora gave him back at his home and gave the walrus $200. "Would this be enough?" he asked, giving the money.

"Sure," said the walrus. "I'll be honored to save anybody's life." He shook Tehran's hand with his front flipper. "So tell me, where can I find Tsarina Abmora?"

"Uh," said Tehran, "she said she'd be somewhere in Canada. Meet me in Toronto."

"Gotcha," said the walrus. He closed the door. Tehran went back to the elevator and pressed the up button and the button marked "2". He went back to his hotel room and back to bed.

CHAPTER 11

Next Stop, Canada

The next morning arrived. Things could get quite colder. Tehran commanded everyone to pack up and get ready for the next stop on the trip, Toronto, Ontario, Canada. They finished surrounding Lake Erie, now was their time to cross the bridge over Niagara Falls.

"We're almost in Canada, Sarah," said Whip.

"Perfect timing for my new suit," said Pition.

They crossed many miles of the bridge. After they made it to the other end, Tehran said, "Our next stop is Toronto."

Everyone looked outside the windows of the motor home. There was much thick snow everywhere.

"We're definitely not in Virginia anymore," said Whip.

"There's not usually that much snow in our place," said Sarah.

Nature existed around the landscape; wolves, bears, and deer were found walking in the surrounding snow. Tall trees and cold creeks existed next to the road. As the Psys, Bobi, and Pition got to Toronto, Tehran parked the motor home in a parking space in front of the city. Everyone walked out. Tehran commanded them to group together, so he could take a picture in a snow patch. Pition felt comfortable in his new slide-through suit.

"This is totally fitting," he said.

Tehran activated his camera, winding it up saying, "Okay, smile, everyone." He was about to press the snapshot button. As he did, Sarah made a face by widening her eyes and shooting out her sticky tongue.

"Sarah, no faces," said Tehran, after he took the picture. "We need smiles, nice ones."

As he took the next picture, Sarah made an evil grin with her eyes barely open.

"Sarah, I said a *nice* smile," said Tehran.

"I *smiled,*" said Sarah.

"I see you were grinning," said Tehran. He wound up the camera again and then said, "I don't much film left, so stop making faces when I take the picture, I need to save some film for other things. You could have been done for the last two minutes, now give a nice smile and hold it for a few seconds." Sarah followed her father's instruction as he took the picture. Sarah kept the smile.

"There, perfect," said Tehran. "Much better." Everyone separated. Corbin went by her husband.

"Don't you think you could earn more money on some larger photo exhibitions, Teh?" she asked.

"Nah, I won't worry," said Tehran. "Our families can treasure this picture." He took the picture and his camera back into the motor home.

CHAPTER 12

The Tree Stooges

Whip, Bobi, and Pition ran their club's next meeting (the "Whip Fan Club").

"This meeting of the Whip Fan Club is now in session," Whip started. "Vice President Bobert Gatorson will give our financial report."

"Okay, as we are undoubtedly aware," said Bobi, "we can sense coldness out here in the woods. We reptiles are cold-blooded, so how can't anyone be aware of extreme coldness?"

"Good question," said Whip. "Vice President Pition Vipers, proceed."

"Hold on, I have a question," said Pition as he was called on. "Doesn't our club have an anthem?"

"You know, I haven't thought about that yet," said Whip. "We'll figure it out some other time. Do your thing."

"Right," said Pition. "It is all because God gave us, reptiles, cold blood, probably because we are monstrous, creepy creatures that used to scare humans in the past. But, those early humans must have taken their own fears everywhere they *went!*" He made that crazy discussion in a higher tone of voice.

"Very nice," said Whip. "Until friendly reptiles choose to be a friendly pet, they will always be allowed. Meeting adjourned."

"Man, what a great club," said Bobi. "Bad enough we don't have very many members."

"Maybe we should get Gavin and Scoobert to join," said Pition.

Suddenly, a call out in the forest occurred, "WHIP!" It was Sarah, loafing around.

"Sarah!" Whip said as he heard the called. He ran to where she was in the forest. He found his sister behind a rock, watching a herd of deer. The deer were prancing and some were mating.

"I never thought about wonderful creatures, making out like that," said Sarah.

"Yeah," said Whip, "life contains excitement, along with the interest in the right person of the opposite gender."

"That's pretty weird," said Sarah.

"You might get attached with that when you're older," said Whip.

"Hey, Whip!" Bobi called. "Check this out, I have found a little cave up there!"

Whip ran to Bobi and Pition and then he found them in front of a tree with a hole far above.

"That's a squirrel hole, guys," said Whip.

"Yeah, right," said Pition. "It can also be used by an owl."

"Let's do a busted move, shall we?" said Bobi. He packed some snow into a ball. He was about to throw it up to the hole.

"Uh, Bobi," said Whip. He didn't think it was a good idea. But Bobi threw it up anyway.

The ball splattered when it hit the top of the cave's mouth. All of a sudden, the splat accidentally woke up a swarm of bats. They flew down to Whip, Bobi, and Pition. Whip went right while Bobi and Pition went left to camp. Whip went to get Sarah while the bat chase was on. Sarah screamed and ran far away to somewhere safe in the front town of Toronto. Whip leaped into a cave by the deer, avoiding the bats as they all flew straight away. As Whip walked out of the cave, he went the other way to look for Sarah. Her footprints led to the old shack town in front of Toronto.

CHAPTER 13

Meet Fentruck Tusker

Whip walked a long way to the town for his sister. There was no sign of Sarah. Whip ended up in front of an old, wooden shack restaurant.

"Sarah!" Whip tried calling his sister inside. Inside was a walrus with a group of walking oyster clams (Sounds like another edition of *Through the Looking Glass*). As the walrus heard Whip's voice, he went to the front room as Whip walked through the doorway.

"Look out there, young man!" the walrus warned Whip. "There's a trap right there in front of you."

"A trap?" said Whip. "Thanks, man." He stepped to the wall and sidled to the other side. "Hi, my name is Whip Psy. I'm looking for a young female of my species named, *Sarah* Psy. She's my sister. Have you seen her?"

"No I haven't," said the walrus. "Hi, my name is Fentruck Tusker."

"Fentruck Tusker?" Whip said. "Well, I'm certainly glad to know you."

"I'm looking for a white ruling tigress called, Abmora Satvrinski. Have you seen her?"

"Uh, no, apparently not."

"We better take a look at this trap." They both walked around for Fentruck Tusker to show the trap behind the door.

"Hey, Mr. Tusker," said Whip, "is there really such a white tigress as Abmora Satvrinski."

"Of course, there is," said Fentruck.

"There is?" said Whip.

"Yep, she is the tsarina of Siberia in Russia; she is also the ruler of the minds of those who are ignorant."

"Wow, lucky I'm smart."

"So I have a trap here with loose wood set for her."

Meanwhile, Sarah was outside until she found that wooden restaurant.

"Hello," she said, opening the door.

In the back of the restaurant with tables, Fentruck walking in between rows, Whip said, "You know, I need you to help me find my family's camp out there."

"Why, are you really that lost?" asked Fentruck.

Suddenly, the trap was activated.

"The trap! The trap!" Fentruck shouted. "Boys, get over there!" He commanded his walking oysters to follow him to the trap. Whip went with them. As they got to the trap, some oysters lowered a net into the hole.

"You know something?" said Fentruck to Whip. "That's the first supreme foreign ruler ever captured by an intelligent animal."

The oysters pulled and pulled.

"Is she powerful?" asked Whip.

"Well, we don't know," said Fentruck.

The oysters got the net up to the real floor. As they did, they found an unknown creature. It was Whip's sister. She crawled out of the net. The oysters ran away from fright.

"It's Sarah!" said Whip. He walked to the net his sister crawled out of. "Sarah! Where have you been? I've walked a long way here, looking for you."

"I only came here because of the bats," said Sarah.

"Bats??" said Fentruck.

"Yeah, we were chased by bats when one of my friends threw a snowball at a tree hole," said Whip.

"Well, you've come to the right place for shelter," said Fentruck.

"Who's this walrus?" Sarah asked her brother.

"This is Fentruck Tusker," said Whip.

"*What* Tusker??" Sarah asked.

"Fen…truck," Whip said.

"Never thought of *that* name before."

"Well you should have that in mind now," said Fentruck. "Boys set the trap again and get it all ready." He commanded his oysters. So they reset the trap.

Later, they sat at a table in the back of the restaurant. Fentruck's partner, Crow Buck (a crow), flew to Fentruck and said, "Fentruck, your oysters are finished resetting your trap."

"Good," said Fentruck.

"I'm sorry I fell in your trap," said Sarah.

"Oh, that's alright," said Fentruck.

Suddenly, the security camera focused on Sarah and shone a laser on her head. When Whip noticed it, he shouted to the security, "Hey you! Will you leave my sis…?!" The camera then focused on Whip. He covered his eyes when the laser shone on him.

"What's gotten into the security people?" asked Sarah.

"I have no idea," said Whip.

"My mind feels numb," said Sarah.

"I better take her back to our site," Whip said to Fentruck.

"I think you better, too," said Fentruck.

"We'll see you later, Fentruck," said Whip.

As Whip and Sarah walked out of the restaurant, Crow Buck had a thought, "Oh," he said, flying down to them, "I think you'll need this." He gave Whip a card, handing it with his foot. The card was a key to Abmora's palace. It could be slid through a sensor slot.

And so, Whip and Sarah walked out of the front town and back to their family's campsite through the frozen valley, heading near the forest and to get some sleep in tents by the motor home. Whip slid the card in his coat.

Whoever was controlling the camera at the restaurant was Aborabor. He left the restaurant and went into the neighboring building next to it. He spoke with his mother and they created a portal to their nation of Russia, to trick the Psy family into their plans.

CHAPTER 14

The Portal to Russia

The Satvrinskis' plans were being made easy. Abmora decided to make contact with Tehran. As her trap was set, she grabbed a nearby phone and dialed Tehran's cell phone number. When Tehran's cell phone rang that morning, he answered it, "Hello."

"Tehran," Abmora said. "I've got it planned. Your daughter's psychiatry shall be quicker this way. She meets spirits in an enchanted pit. She'll have all the wisdom she'll ever need."

"Alright," said Tehran. "Where are you?"

"I'm in the top room in the Saloon on Ice Street in front of Toronto in this old town," said Abmora.

"I'll be there," said Tehran. He packed all the camping stuff in the motor home.

When Whip had heard the call he grabbed the card key to Abmora's palace out of his jacket and looked at it, turning it to view the opposite side. He put the card back in his jacket's pocket. He got up and dressed for the day. He jumped out of the motor home and went to Bobi and Pition's tent.

"Guys," he said trying to wake them up.

"Whip?" Bobi got up. "Where have you been last night?"

"I had to get my sister from fright of those bats, chasing us," said Whip. "We ended up in this restaurant with a walrus and his friend gave me this card for a secret place to go to."

"Fabulous," said Pition, trying to wake up.

"Pack up this tent, guys," said Whip. "My dad has another place to go."

The boys packed their stuff as Pition put on his slide-through suit. Bobi dressed himself and put on his warm fur jacket. They folded the tent, removing the rods out of the frame. They packed everything in the back of the motor home. And so, Tehran drove to Toronto's old front shack town. He thought about psychiatry for the while he drove. Sarah obviously could use a self-diaper change in the motor home's bathroom.

As they were in the right place, Tehran had to speak with the Satvrinskis in the upper room of the building next to the restaurant containing Fentruck and his buddies. Whip found a card slot next to the fireplace. He pulled the card that Crow Buck gave him, out of his jacket pocket. He looked at it and read, "Key Card to the Tsarina's Portal." He was about to walk toward the fireplace to insert and slide the card until he suddenly heard steps thumping on the stairs down. He hid under the table with his friends. Abmora and Aborabor came downstairs to the fireplace flu and Abmora slid her card through the sensor slot and the Satvrinskis vanished into the magic green dust.

Whip got the idea. "Are you guys up for a little quest?" he asked his friends. He knew at once that his father finished the conversation with those white tigers.

"Well I believe so," said Bobi.

"I'm leaving a note," said Whip. He wrote: I've found a clue in the fireplace. –Whip

Then the three boys stepped toward the fireplace. Whip slid the card through the sensor slot. A green mist appeared and sparkled.

"Wow," said Bobi. "A mystic portal."

"I spy magic," said Pition.

"This must be the portal to Abmora Satvrinski's palace," said Whip. "We must follow her and her son there."

"We're on a discovery," said Bobi. And the boys entered the fireplace and vanished in the green mist.

Meanwhile, the rest of the Psy family came downstairs by the fireplace. They noticed that the boys had disappeared. Tehran had just spotted the note that his son left.

"I've found a clue in the fireplace. –Whip," Tehran read the note.

"I wonder where he is now," said Corbin.

33

"Maybe he *disappeared* in the fireplace," said Sarah. "That's what he meant."

"I don't think so, Sarah," said Tehran. He turned to look to the fireplace and suddenly noticed a card slot on the left side. He pulled his credit card out of his briefcase and slid it through the sensor. A green mist appeared and wrote: ACCESS DENIED. The new mystery was discovered, according to Tehran's thoughts.

CHAPTER 15

Abmora's Palace

As Whip, Bobi, and Pition reappeared from the green mist into a snowy plain in Siberia, Russia, Whip modified one of his thoughts, "It's hard to believe that some kids have to use diapers because they can't control their bladders."

"Yeah," said Bobi. "It was pretty shocking to see those diapers in the special education students' bathroom."

"I think pregnant women should use diapers because their uteri, holding a baby, squish their bladders," said Whip.

"Suffice to say," said Pition, "not all females prefer to use diapers. Most worldly animals lay eggs as we know."

"Yeah," said Whip. "Let's just end this edifying conversation, there's something likely to be exotic that we must find."

As the three boys set off through the frozen forest and tundra, they witnessed a large, fancy palace that reminded them of a historical U.S.S.R. building.

"Whoa, man!" Bobi cried. "That looks like the home of Czar Nicholas II."

"That must be Tsarina Abmora Satvrinski's palace," said Pition.

"Looks like our quest has just begun," said Whip.

"Has it now?" said Bobi. So the boys stepped on and hit the path to the spiral-domed, purple-painted palace. They made it to the two large, wooden and brass doors. Whip grabbed one of the rings and knocked. A hatch above them opened up and a security camera came out.

"You may enter," it said with a mechanical tone of voice.

Whip opened the doors and the boys walked in. As they did, they saw a purple desk with a white owl sitting at it. The boys walked toward him.

"Hi," said Whip to the owl. "We're here to see Tsarina…"

"…Abmora Satvrinski," said the owl, finishing Whip's thought. "I'm sorry. She's not in yet."

"Lagon," said a voice through the loudspeaker to the owl. It was Abmora. "Come with the mail order to the office. NOW!"

The owl sighed. He pressed the speaker button and said, "Yes, your majesty! Right away." He turned to the three boys and said, "Look, she's not interested to meet with any client today. Okay?"

"That's fine, dude," said Whip. "Besides, we're from the other side of the world."

"Other side of the world?" said the owl.

"Yeah," said Whip. "These friends of mine are real, but I'm a myth. Just be lucky that animals aren't prejudice, only humans are."

The owl nodded his head, "Mm-hm."

"So I guess we're just gonna have a look around." Whip was just about to walk deeper in the palace with his friends. Then he turned back to the owl and said, "Oh, by the way. Would it be easy enough if the Tsarina didn't know we were here? Know what I'm saying? Huh?"

"Hm?" said Bobi.

"Huh?" Whip said again.

"Huh? Huh? Huh…??!" Pition moved his head in various emotions while talking to the owl.

"Stop it," Whip said to Pition.

"Of course," said the owl. "Go right in."

And so, the boys walked into the door behind the owl's desk. They found purple stone hallways with lamps lighting the dark.

"What a creepy place this is," said Pition.

"There are subtitles on the doors," said Bobi.

"Good," said Whip. "We need to find the throne room." So the boys read every sign on every door. This took a long time until down the left hall, Whip found a pair of two large purple doors, framed with brass bars. The sign read "Throne Room".

"Guys!" Whip called to his friends. "I found it!" Bobi and Pition arrived to his position.

"Happy day," said Bobi.

Whip opened the door slowly. He saw a white tigress through a thin opening that he made with the door. It was Abmora, creating a new potion for the plan with Sarah Psy's education. She noticed the thin opening in the doors away from her throne.

"Come in," she said.

Whip opened the door. Then he and his friends walked across the long red runner with golden batons.

Abmora concentrated on the potion's recipe, "Brain food to the young ones." She added shreds of canned fish to the concoction.

Just as the boys approached, Abmora stopped her mixture and set the wooden spoon aside. Then she noticed a strange, familiar creature, while staring at Whip.

"Sorry to barge in like this, but…" Whip said.

"What do you seek about me?" asked Abmora.

"Well," said Whip. "I can tell that my father has been talking to you lately. And…I think you need professional assistance on your plan."

"I don't need assistance right now," said Abmora. "I'm a highly educated tigress. I can tell you by such a mythical creature never told before like you." She stared at Whip, studying him.

"Well…yeah, but I don't mean *actual* assistance. I mean you should redefine your plan in a better way for my sister."

"I know what I'm doing!" Abmora shouted in vain. Bobi and Pition panicked.

Suddenly, a puffin arrived with a rolling cart of food for the Tsarina.

"Lots of salmon, lots…" he said. Whip, Bobi, and Pition turned behind themselves.

"Oh," said the puffin. "Heh heh, sorry."

"Uh," said Whip. "That's fine. We were just about to leave." He turned back to Abmora and said, "We're awfully sorry to have wasted your time, your majesty."

"Just…" said Abmora, "go." She lifted her paw and opened it in front of herself.

"Come on, guys," Whip called to his friends. So they left the throne room.

As they walked back to the hall, Whip's next plan was to find a potion that would help his species. All his magical thoughts moved through his head.

"Follow me, guys," he called to his friends.

As they followed him, Bobi asked, "What's your next plan?"

"We're looking for the potion room," said Whip.

"What for?" asked Bobi.

We have to find a better idea for my species' wisdom," said Whip. "The tsarina is planning to manipulate my sister." The boys searched for the potion room, walking through the hallway back to the other end until, at the very end, they found the potion room. They entered it and Whip plotted the plan. "Bobi, make yourself useful and go keep watch." Bobi did Whip's bidding. "Pition," Whip said on the next part of his plan. "Do you think you can get to those on top? 'Cause one of those has got to help."

"Sure thing, Whip," said Pition. "If only I can flip myself up from shelf to shelf."

Bobi cleared his throat and said, "Whip, this is a bad idea. 'Cause I don't think that tsarina woman will let us have any of these."

"Bobi," said Whip. "Keep watch."

"Yeah, don't worry, I will," said Bobi. He pressed his head to one of the doors nearly opening it. He peaked through the thin opening.

As Pition swung up the shelves, he asked Whip what potions were necessary, "Earwax Sculptability?"

"Oh yeah, right, I had to clean someone's ears," said Bobi, "but not to sculpt it."

"Mythology?" asked Pition upon another potion.

"If you want," said Whip.

"I'm interested!" shouted Bobi. Pition grabbed the small flask of the Mythology potion with his tail and tossed it down into Bobi's hands cupped together. The flask landed directly into them. Pition continued searching.

"At least *I'm* already mythological," said Whip.

"Lava Stomach?" Pition asked among another potion.

"U-uh," said Whip.

"Omega Lax?" Pition asked upon another potion.

"No." Whip pressed his face against his hand. Then he circled his fingers in front of his mouth and said, "Try 'Greatest Wisdom'."

Pition swung to a shelf beside him and looked around others. "Sorry, no 'Greatest Wisdom'," he said. He climbed and climbed, until at the top beside sealing glass, he discovered a rectangular flask of gold liquid. "Hey!" he called down to Whip. "How about 'Eternal Life'?"

"Well," said Whip, "what's it say?"

"It says, 'For this immortal life, all sins are forgiven and ye shall have obtained the drink from the Fountain of Youth'."

"You know, eternal life is the greatest gift from God," said Bobi, "according to what I read about Mormons."

Suddenly, animals outside in the hall snitched on the open door to the potion room. Whip gasped when he noticed them, "Uh-h, Bobi!"

Bobi turned to the outside and shrieked when he closed the door.

"Better hurry!" Whip called up to Pition. "We got company!"

Pition put his whole body on the shelf with the wooden crate with glass walls. He opened his mouth, unhooking his jaws. His mouth went very wide. He pressed his teeth on the glass wall in front of him. Then he twisted his neck side by side to cut a circle in the glass. Then he rehooked his and head-butted the circle he carved. He grabbed the rectangular flask of the Eternal Life potion in his mouth and jumped backward off the highest shelf. He fell. Bobi opened his jaws under Pition to catch him. Pition fell in his mouth.

"Nice catch, Bobi," said Whip.

"You better not eat me," said Pition to Bobi.

"I won't," said Bobi with Pition in his mouth.

Suddenly, potions started to fall and their flasks broke. The alarm of emergencies rang. The boys fled the potion room. They ran down the hall across a band of guards raising their weapons in front of the boys. Whip ran on a wall around them. Bobi chomped to scare the guards away. He held Pition around his arm and Bobi broke away, ramming the guards with his head and shoving them away. He caught up with Whip. They grabbed shields from suits of armor displayed on pedestals. They surfed on the shields across the hall among steel balls and chains blocking their path through the exit. As they made it through a high gold closing gate, they turned into the front office where they met in the first place. They jumped off the shields they were surfing on. Pition was knocked off of Bobi's arm. He spewed the potion from his mouth. Whip caught it.

"Gotcha!" he said. The boys exited the palace.

Meanwhile, Abmora investigated the halls. The guards gathered their weapons.

"Look, I don't care whose fault it is, just get this place organized this instant!" Abmora yelled in front of a few puffins.

"Yes, your majesty," the puffins said and they flew around the hall to stack armor correctly on each pedestal.

"And someone bring me a fish with its guts smothered in spaghetti," said Abmora.

Suddenly, Aborabor opened the doors from the front office and entered the hallway, shouting, "Mother!"

"Aborabor," said Abmora, confronting her son. "This is no time to confess, pumpkin, your mother's busy."

"Well, well," said Aborabor, looking around the hall, "what happened here?"

"Whip Psy and his friends messed around this whole place," said Abmora.

"What?!?" shouted Aborabor. "Where are those intruders? I shall pounce on them wherever they stand. They will rue the very day they stole my kingdom from me!" He pressed his fists against the sides of his head.

"Oh, keep it quiet, sonny, you're still going to be tsar," said Abmora. "We'll just have to outsmart Whip and that's all."

Suddenly the white owl from the front office approached Abmora as he held a parchment of the incident. He cleared his throat and said, "Pardon?" Abmora turned to him.

"Everything is quite organized like it should be, your majesty," the owl said, "e-except for two…potions."

"What??" Abmora grabbed the parchment from the owl's talons. "Oh," she said. "I do believe we can modify this unexpected crime in one easy step." She thought of her plan, suffering on welcoming the three heroes.

CHAPTER 16

The Potions' Process

As Whip, Bobi, and Pition traveled through the tundra away from the palace, they read about the potions of how they work.

"Eternal life," Whip read the Eternal Life potion. "For all believers in the name of God, one who drinks from the fountain shall obtain the greatest gift of all."

"A drink from the fountain'??" said Bobi. "That's ridiculous. I wouldn't even imagine having to drink gold water like that. So just drop that jar of voodoo and let's get out of here!"

"It says 'the greatest gift of all'!" said Whip. "How bad can it possibly be?" He unplugged the open top of the flask and smelled the potion. It smelled like powerful vinegar. Whip exhaled the smell, panicking.

"Ah ha," Bobi laughed. "Let's see what *this* potion says." He read the Mythology potion's inscription: "This magic gift is to help relate to whatever mythical beast was told about."

"Maybe if there's something wrong with that potion," said Pition, "allow me to take the first sip."

"Go ahead, Pit, help yourself," said Bobi, handing the flask of the Mythology potion to Pition. Pition grabbed the flask with his tail, and then he foiled his mouth around the open mouth of the flask and dumped the potion into his mouth and down his esophagus. He drank half of the potion. Then he took his mouth off the flask and handed it back to Bobi.

"How do you feel?" Whip asked Pition.

"Uh...fine. I'm a bit queasy," said Pition shaking his body for a second.

"Don't worry," said Bobi. "Let a professional croc show you how it's done." He opened his mouth halfway and dumped the remaining half of the potion down his esophagus as he swallowed it. "Aaahhh!" he sighed as he finished.

"How do you feel, Bobi?" Whip asked.

"Well, I don't feel any different at all," said Bobi. "Do I *look* any different?"

"You're still the same old crocodile, Bobe," said Pition.

"Maybe it doesn't work for a while on you guys," said Whip. He raised the Eternal Life potion and then said, "I'll have to give *this* one a try."

"Whoa, hey, Whip!" Bobi shouted to him. "Your drinking that means no dying."

"I know," said Whip.

"Yeah, but..." said Bobi, "no changing when you grow older?"

"I *know.*"

"And no more doing wrong?"

"I know!"

"But you love livin'..."

"I KNOW!" Whip shouted. "But as long as I live, people will always remember me, and they'll never deny me. I'll be the best myth ever told." He put the flask to his lips and started drinking.

"Whip!" Bobi shouted. "No! Wait!"

Whip continued drinking. As he finished, Whip started to feel bubbles in his stomach. He felt sick. Bobi and Pition hid behind a nearby rock. Whip felt something run up his esophagus. He started to burp for a few seconds. After it ended, Bobi and Pition came out of hiding behind the rock.

"Man, Whip," said Bobi. "I think you drank a 'Belch-ternal Life' potion."

"Maybe something's wrong with it and that's why it made you burp," said Pition.

"Well, I guess it was worth it," said Whip, "and I wasn't meant to do this thing."

Suddenly, a cold wind started to howl and blow specks of snow. Bobi shivered. Pition tucked himself in his slide-through suit.

"Alright I'm cold-blooded in a cold wind," said Bobi.

"We're lucky we have something warm to put on," said Pition.

"Relax, guys," said Whip. "It will last shortly."

So the three boys walked the path back to the portal they went through in the first place. The cold wind continued to blow. As Whip slid the card through the portal, the green mist appeared and the boys went through it and they warped back to the log cabin where they started. Night came by and the boys tried to find a place to sleep. Suddenly, Pition fell asleep on the floor.

"Pition?" Whip noticed. "Are you awake?"

"Man," said Bobi, "that's how *I* feel, too." He fell asleep, falling on the floor next to Pition.

"Bobi?" said Whip. "G-guys." He fell forward and asleep on Bobi. The potions must have had an effect which made them asleep until the following morning.

Meanwhile, back at the Psys' camp with the motor home, they were thoughtful of missing Whip.

"I just can't believe our son and his friends would disappear in a distance like this," said Tehran, looking out the window of the motor home.

Corbin, in her brown and tan striped sweater, approached her husband, saying, "Sometimes, it's like those who are old enough to wander in the wilderness."

Sarah suddenly approached behind her parents, wearing her pink snow trousers. Tehran turned to her and said, "There you are. We missed you at dinner."

"Where have you been, Sarah?" Corbin asked.

"I had thoughts about what's going on with us in this place," said Sarah. "I think I'm going out to find Whip and his pals." She grabbed her jacket and headed for the side door.

"Sarah?!" Corbin called to her.

"You can't go out there, it's too cold at night," said Tehran.

As Sarah opened the door, something washed through her head and she fell to the snowy ground from the door's steps. Her parents bent down and lifted her from the snow and took her back in the motor home. Tehran closed the door with his foot.

Meanwhile, back at the old log cabin, Whip, Bobi, and Pition dreamed deep as they slept. As they did a magical beam began to rise amongst them and explode. Bobi and Pition turned into mythical beasts. Whip was affected by a golden beam granting his eternal life. He did not quite feel it.

Back at the motor home, Tehran and Corbin tucked their daughter in the large bed in the middle of the vehicle's body. Suddenly, as the parents sat in chairs nearby, they automatically fell asleep, because their son had drunk the Eternal Life potion. Things were about to change.

CHAPTER 17

Things Are Changing

The next morning, a group of puffins surrounded Whip as he was still asleep but wide awake. The puffins were two males and two females.

"Hello," said a female puffin to Whip, still sleeping. "Are you awake?" She patted her wing on Whip's hip. Whip woke up screaming.

"MORNING!" shouted all the puffins.

Whip lifted himself up and exhaled sharply. "What is going on here?"

A male puffin said, "We saw you sleeping in our cabin on the floor with this demon snake."

"Demon snake??" Whip heard the words and said them. "What do you mean?"

The other male puffin stood next to Pition, now a strange, yellow-dotted, black-diamond back, horn-nosed snake. The puffin said, "How do you stand having an ugly creature like this as your roommate?"

"Pition?" Whip asked.

"Yeah, it's me," said Pition, lifting his triangular bladed tail.

"This has got to be a dream," said Whip.

"Here," said the other female puffin, grabbing a nearby mug of water, "I filled you up some water to wake you up."

"Uh-hh…thanks," Whip yawned. He reached the mug and suddenly witnessed a golden glow, replacing his shadow. He grabbed the mug to see his reflection in the water. Golden light filled the mug. Whip saw that his reflection was normal, but something was wrong with his shadow. He dropped the mug and it spilled the water. He figured that the bright, golden shadow would light up in the dark.

"This *has* to be a dream," he said. "Instead of a black shadow, I have a bright shadow. I…I'm…"

"Mystical, I'll say," said one of the male puffins.

"My name's Sherbet," said one of the females. "What's yours?"

"Uh…Whip," said Whip.

"Whip? Wow," said the other female puffin.

"Where are you from?" asked one of the males.

"America," said Whip. "Has anybody seen a crocodile?"

"Who're you calling 'crocodile'?!" Bobi called from outside. As Whip found him out the door, Bobi appeared to be an emerald dragon.

"Bobi?" said Whip. "You're a…"

"A dragon, man!" Bobi shouted with excitement. "I can breathe fire." He spewed a giant fireball towards the downhill road of the village. "I can fly." He flapped his wings and reached for the sky, pointing to it with his snout. "Look at me, Whip!" he dove back down to the snowy ground. "I'm pretty enchanting, aren't I?" He landed. "That's some quality potion. I wonder what's in it."

Pition slithered to the doorway. He grabbed the two potion flasks with his tail and read the back label of the Mythology potion:

"Warning: Side effects can cause confusion, brain damage, poor vision, and DNA blunders will occur during the transformation."

"Wow," said Bobi. "I can't even feel any brain damage."

"Well I can," said Pition, feeling overwhelmed with a headache.

"What about the Eternal Life?" asked Whip.

"Oh right," said Pition. He quickly snatched the eternal life potion's flask and read the back label, saying, "To make the effect of this potion last, the drinker must do things that are good in order to accomplish the gift before midnight."

Whip grabbed the flask out of Pition's coil grip.

"Midnight?!" he said. "What kind of nonsense are we going for?"

"I don't think it's nonsense," said a male puffin. "You probably should go for whatever it depends on."

"Look. Puffins," said Whip. "I can figure this out okay."

"Okay, never mind," said the male puffin.

"Let's say," said Pition. "You have until midnight to promise you'll live forever."

"Right," said Whip.

"Ya know, we might look different," said Bobi. "But inside, you, Whip, are the same genius-powered, incredible, mythical psyvark you've always been."

"And you're still the same crazy crocodile," said Whip.

"Yeah," said Bobi.

"And I guess I'm the same stubborn snake," said Pition.

"Well," said Whip. "Look out everyone. Here come the new us." He raised his fist but unexpectedly made a glow between his fingers.

"And, one more thing," said Bobi. "You better hide your glowing powers."

The puffins giggled.

Whip, Bobi, and Pition exit the cabin. As they felt the snow under them, Whip hopped on Bobi's back and Pition coiled his body around Bobi's tail. Bobi flapped his new webbed wings and started hovering in midair. The three friends flew over the town, searching for Whip's family.

"WAHOO!" Whip shouted.

After a long search, there was no sign of the Psy family. Whip thought if they were out looking for him. Suddenly, Whip's mind gained a thought. He read it, saying that his father was to interrogate with Abmora about Sarah's lack of true education.

"Of course," said Whip. "Bobi," he moved his snout over Bobi's dragon ear saying, "I think my family's talking with the tsarina at her palace." So the three friends flew a shortcut around the Arctic Circle from Canada to Siberia. Bobi must be too big to fit back in the fireplace portal.

After a long morning, Whip and his pals finally got to Siberia to land near the Satvrinskis' palace. Whip ran up to the entrance, confronting the guards and he said, "I'm here to speak with your ruler." But one of the guards did not understand English.

Meanwhile, inside the palace, the Psy family seemed invisible for a while. Tehran and Corbin spoke with the tsarina. Sarah was upstairs in the bathroom washing her face.

"SARAH!" Whip called out.

When Sarah heard the call, she opened the window over the fancy couch. She saw Whip. As Whip saw her, he dismounted Bobi and ran up the porch steps, opening the door and he looked for his sister. He ran up the foyer stairs. Sarah started looking for her brother. She ran out of the current room she was in. Whip ran to the left from the top step. Sarah ran down the foyer stairs. Whip suddenly ended up in a room of bookcases and couches. He saw a black pillar, standing by the window. Whip studied it and spotted the tail of a white tiger.

"Hello there," it was Abmora turning around to face Whip.

Meanwhile, Sarah headed out the front door. She called out, "Whip!"

"Morning, Sarah!" Bobi called from nearby.

Sarah turned to him with astonishment.

"Bobi?" she wondered.

"Yeah, I look different, don't I?" Bobi said.

"What happened to you guys?"

"It's kind of a long story, you see, Whip, Pition, and I took these magic potions and now…we're *sexy!* Aren't we, Pit?" Bobi looked back at Pition lying on his back.

"I've been feeling ill this morning," Pition said.

"Yeah, he's been down lately," said Bobi.

"Bobi, where is my brother?!" Sarah asked abruptly.

"He just went inside looking for you," Bobi answered. Sarah ran back to the front door up the porch's steps.

"Whip!" she called.

When Whip heard the call, he tried to run out of the current room he was in, but Abmora suddenly waved her scepter to shut and lock the doors.

"Hey!" Whip shouted. "I'm trying to get to my sister." He ran to an open balcony, and Abmora shut its doors, too.

"How can you be going to her that way?" she asked. "You should come to these windows and see for yourself."

Sarah looked around for Whip. Suddenly, she heard a voice she hadn't heard before that said, "Hello, Sarah." It was Aborabor. Sarah turned to him.

"Who are you?" she asked.

"My name is Aborabor Satvrinski," he introduced himself.

"Aborabor *what??*" Sarah asked again.

"Sat-vrin-ski. It's a Russian name. I suppose it's hard for you to say it at this little age of yours."

Suddenly, the Psy parents found their daughter by the foyer window.

"Sarah!" said Corbin. "There you are."

"Aborabor?" Tehran said as he witnessed Aborabor standing by.

"Ah, do you think so," Aborabor chuckled, "Mr. Psy. I was rather hoping you could prove me."

"And, who are you?" Corbin asked that tiger.

"Oh! Hi, Mrs. Psy," said Aborabor. "I'm Aborabor Satvrinski. My mother is the tsarina. She's making me a specialist with your daughter before I become the new tsar of Siberia. She says that she needs a proper education." As he spoke with the Psys, Whip looked out the window with Abmora next to him.

"Sarah!" he shouted. "Mom, Dad! Don't listen to him!" He shouted and shouted. But no one could hear him through the thick glass window.

"They can't hear you right now," said Abmora. Whip turned away from the window. Abmora continued, "Do you think you'll miss a youthful creature's new life?"

"I just wanted her to learn some manners," Whip sighed.

"Well now, I believe she can," said Abmora. "She's going to get a proper education just like you."

"But look at me," said Whip. "How can I live my life for my family?"

"It's just time you lived in a myth, Whip. She's a young female, and you're a teenage male. That is one thing that may often change in your juvenile years."

Whip turned back to the window and saw his family leave the balcony with Aborabor.

"Well," he said. "I tried to love her."

"If that is true," said Abmora, "you should let us babysit her."

And so, Whip walked out of the palace, passing by his friends on the path walk.

"Hey, Whip," they both said.

"How'd it go?" asked Pition. Whip walked by Bobi's front end.

"Hey, what's going on?" Bobi asked Whip. "Where're ya goin'?!" He and Pition followed Whip around the snowy fields. Far later, they ended up in an old billiards shack called, Lao Mushu's Bar.

CHAPTER 18

Under Arrest

As the boys entered Lao Mushu's Bar, Whip thought about what his family was to go for with the Satvrinskis. They sat at the front counter on stools. Whip set his chin on his fist. A panda bartender served beer at the counter.

"How about it, boys," he said.

"We don't drink," said Whip with his eyes nearly closed.

"Hey," said the bartender. "You look down today, what's the problem?"

"It was all just a stupid idea of my dad's," Whip said, moving his eyes around. "I never should've trusted this vacation."

"I see."

"I can't believe you just walked away from yo' family like that, Whip," said Bobi. "It's just not okay."

Pition exhaled, popping his lips, "I hate it when things turn out like that."

"For how good can it be?" said Whip. "My sister is stuck with those white tigers, the Satvrinskis."

"Are they really that kind of genius?" Bobi asked.

"Are you kidding?" said the bartender. "They're *extreme* geniuses. They have all kinds of educational stuff in their palace."

"Wowzers," said Pition. "Sounds like weirdness."

"You know," said Whip, "occasionally, this is making me feel nervous. Look, guys, it's for the best. My parents talk with those tigers and my sister is going to get some fundamental education. Everybody wins."

"Except for you," said Bobi. "I don't get it, Whip, you're supposed to *love* your sister."

"Yeah, right," said Whip. "That's why I'm letting the tigers babysit her."

Suddenly, Tehran entered the bar under a brown cloak. He went to the serving counter and asked the bartender, "Excuse me. I thought I saw the 'Satvrinskis' enter here..."

"Sure," said the bartender. "They're at the side door." He pointed to the door at Tehran's left, where two polar bear guards stood by. They permitted him to enter the room. As Tehran entered the room, he saw the Satvrinskis.

"So," he said. "Your royal highness Abmora, and Aborabor."

Abmora sighed, "You better have a good reason for the knowledge of your children."

"Well," said Tehran, "it seems that Sarah isn't warming up to the real world."

"Um, P.S.," said Aborabor, "not important. What kind of real world can there be when I had to take care of that little twit?"

"Well it's not very natural of a habit," said Tehran.

"What?!?" the Satvrinskis both asked simultaneously.

"I mean..." Tehran continued. "You can't force anyone to get a good or excellent education."

As they talked, Whip, Bobi, and Pition snuck to the side wall of the bar and sidled to the window.

Abmora chuckled, "It's all part of the game. I do it all the time." She pulled out a small flask of a potion that she invented from her robe, handing it to Tehran. "Have your daughter drink this and she will know to get used to reality during the ceremony or perhaps she will have to die." Whip shrugged when he heard the tsarina talk about the potion.

"Um," said Tehran, "no."

"What did you say?" Abmora asked.

"Well, I can't," said Tehran. "I don't think that's a good idea."

"Oh, nonsense." Abmora raised her golden-shafted, lamp-headed scepter and moved forward to Tehran, saying, "If you remember, I helped you with your knowledge long before you ever knew me. I can take that away just as easily." The head of her scepter glowed as Tehran turned his face from it. "Is that what you want? Is it?? Hmm." She moved a bit more forward.

"Uuugghh," Tehran muttered with his mouth merely open. "Nooo…"

"Good," said Abmora, moving back to her seat. "So we have to go. I'll have to do Aborabor's fur before the ceremony. He's hopeless. He hasn't got a charm in his taste."

"Oh," Aborabor chuckled, "yes indeed, Mother."

"Mother?!?" Bobi shouted from out the window.

"Uh, ma'am," said Whip, "a modern-day dragon."

"THE PERPETRATOR!" Abmora shouted.

Whip, Bobi, and Pition started to run away from Lao Mushu's Bar. Whip and Pition jumped onto Bobi's back. They prepared to charge and fly away. Guards chased after them.

Abmora shouted out in an outrage, "STOP THEM! THIEVES, ROBBERS! SIEZE THEM!" As she ran out of the bar, she zapped a beam from her scepter. The three heroes dodged it. The guards chased the heroes into the cold forest. Tehran came out and he shouted, "NOOO!" As he shouted the guards were still running after the heroes.

"THAT'S MY SON!" Tehran shouted again. Whip, Bobi, and Pition were suddenly placed under arrest.

CHAPTER 19

The Supermental Plan

And so, a ceremony was to be run. The Satvrinskis had planned an evil thing to do with Sarah Psy. This ceremony was plotted with a green misty pit for anyone's brain to absorb education for the future. Abmora said that if Sarah accepts it, she would be smart; but if not, she would be sacrificed forever. As the ceremony was being run, a Russian ball happened inside the Satvrinskis' palace. As a preamble, this was just before the sacrifice. The ball was displayed on TV. Now back at the Psys' house the animals were watching the television in the master bedroom where Tehran and Corbin sleep. The ball was on PBS.

"Man, I hate this ball show!" Slippy the slug shouted out. "It's all boring me to ooze. Let's change it to Comedy Central."

"I'm not flipping anywhere until I see Whip, Bobi, and Pition," said Sampson the seal, lying on the front of the bed on his belly with the remote in his flippers.

"Bah! I'll slime you guys!" said Slippy being angry. He turned his sight to the four fat frogs and said, "Hey, frogs, pass me a popcorn kernel."

The frogs dug in the bowl of popcorn to the bottom for a kernel.

"Hah," said one of the frogs as he found one. "Got one." He pulled himself out of the bowl, and then tossed the kernel to Slippy, who had his mouth open. He caught the kernel and gobbled it up.

When a commercial break happened, Sampson changed the channel to Nickelodeon.

"Are ya ready, kids?!" growled the pirate picture, suddenly happening on the channel.

"Ah, now here's a good show," said Slippy.

"I can't hear you!" growled the pirate on TV.

"Aye aye, captain!" the kids in the background shouted.

The pirate started singing, *"Ohhhhh…"* The TV showed the pineapple under the sea with SpongeBob Squarepants.

The "SpongeBob Squarepants" opening theme went on until suddenly, an interruption happened.

"We interrupt this program to bring you this emergency broadcast," said the announcer.

A news woman announced, "There has been a risk by a modern-day dragon flying over Siberia. Russian polices have reacted among this beast and its riders terrorizing the skies." They showed Whip, Bobi, and Pition being caught.

"Don't arrest me," said Whip. "I'm a hero of this planet."

The camera focused on Bobi in his dragon form, being chained.

"Have mercy!" Bobi shouted. "I'M A FRIENDLY BEAST!"

"I need to get back to my family!" Whip shouted.

The camera focused on Pition in his strange snake form.

"You can't cross me," he said. He jumped at a policeman approaching him. He hissed and coiled around his neck, trying to suffocate him. But other cops grabbed him off. They threw the heroes into a prison van.

"I'm not really a dragon," said Bobi, "I'm a crocodile!"

"No, please…" said Whip as the cops closed the van's back doors. Whip said from behind the window, "We're heroes! My name is Whip Psy! I'm trying to save my family." The van was driven away.

Sampson turned off the TV with the remote.

"Did you guys hear that?" asked Kirbo the cassowary, standing next to the bed.

"That was Whip, Bobi, and Pition," said Sampson. "They're in big trouble!"

"Oh, no!" the four fat frogs croaked.

"We've got to save them!" said Slippy.

"But how?" said Pango the pangolin. "We'll never make it there in time!"

"Indeed not," said Webb the spider. "It's too far away from here."

"I've got it!" said Kirbo. "We'll use the World Bug that Whip built after saving us from our Vip owners."

"Let's go, guys!" Slippy cried out.

So the animals went out of the house and into the garage and found the World Bug. They hopped into it. They drove to the Vipers' house. Kirbo walked out and went to knock on the door. Inside, the Vipers family was eating dinner, for after many months they didn't have to eat. As they heard a knock on the door, Pition's teenage sister, Pennifer, answered the door.

"Whoa!" Pennifer said in astonishment.

"Hi, I'm looking for your brother's pet parrot, Pauley Hangerson," said Kirbo. "We might need him on a mission of search and rescue."

"Well, sure," said Pennifer. "He's a smart aleck alright for you guys." She slithered up to Pition's room and grabbed the dome-topped cage with Pauley Hangerson (P.H.), which is Pition's pet green parrot. Pennifer carried the cage by the top handle in her mouth and slithered downstairs. She went back to the door and set the cage down in front of Kirbo. He reached down to grab the cage's handle in his beak. He walked with it back to the World Bug. P.H. screeched and said, "Going on an adventure."

Kirbo went back into the vehicle and set P.H. on an empty seat between Sampson and Pango. The animals hovered to midair and blasted off to Siberia.

Meanwhile, as nightfall arrived in Siberia, Tehran was making hot chocolate in the palace's kitchen for himself, his wife, and his daughter. As he filled three cups, setting them on a platter, Tehran took out the potion that Abmora gave him and uncorked the flask. He poured it into the cup at the right end of the platter. Then he grabbed the platter and left the kitchen. He found his wife in the lounge.

"Honey?" he said. "I made us some hot chocolate."

"Oh," said Corbin turning to her husband. "Thanks." She grabbed the cup from the left end of the platter.

"I'll find Sarah," said Tehran, leaving the lounge. He walked up the stairs of the foyer and found Sarah in a room with a wide window. Sarah sat on the couch in front of the window.

"Sarah?" Tehran said as he entered the room, opening the door. "Ah," he said as he found his daughter on the couch. "I thought I might find you here. How about a nice hot cup of chocolate before the ceremony?"

"I don't want to go," said Sarah.

"Oh b-but…" Tehran chuckled as he set the platter on a nearby small table. "These white tigers want you to get smart so you can get better grades in school."

"There's just one problem," said Sarah, "Whip's not here. I mean I'm stuck with these tigers." She pointed to Aborabor down below from the window. Aborabor was showing his ways of appealing to the crowd.

"Well," said Tehran, "yes, they are kind of strangers. But…sometimes people at Whip's age are old enough to go out in other places; like, I would go other places with your mother."

"Going places?" Sarah exhaled and then said, "They've completely lost their minds."

"Well, nonsense. You might find that you'll be smart just like anybody else."

"But the only thing that would make me feel smart is my brother, Whip." Sarah slid off the couch. "I'd do anything to see him again." She walked to the small table to reach a cup of hot chocolate at the far right end of the platter.

"Uh-uh, sweetie!" Tehran caught her as he noticed. "That's mine." He grabbed the cup on the right. "To sleep…otherwise I'm up all night."

Sarah grabbed the remaining cup and took a sip. She felt warm inside her throat as she drank the hot chocolate.

CHAPTER 20

Prison Break

And so, Whip, Bobi, and Pition were locked in a prison upon the snowy plains of Siberia. They were shackled on a wall above the ground. Whip hung by his wrists. Bobi hung by his wrists and ankles. Pition hung by his neck and his tail.

Bobi screamed aloud, "No one is to prosecute me! I'm a nice dragon in this form! What about our families?! You're to say, I have the right to feel confident! Nobody said I have the right to feel confident!"

"Bobi, you *do* have the right to feel confident," Whip told him. "What you have is complete righteousness in your life with capacity."

"I should coil myself before anyone kills me," Pition whimpered.

Suddenly, youthful, scarped voices called down to them from the roof through a barred hole, "Whip?! Bobi?? Pition?!?" It was the animals who arrived from our heroes' hometown.

"Oh well," said Pition.

"Slippy! Webb! P.H!" Whip called up to the animals. "Get us out of here!"

One of the four fat frogs lit a match on fire to light the fuse of one of the dynamite sticks that the animals placed on the bar frame. But the frog fell in the dungeon. Pango the pangolin lit another match.

"Fire in the hole!" he shouted. "Everyone clear out!" He lit the fuses of the dynamite sticks. The animals backed away for the sticks to explode. So they did. The bars fell apart and the hole turned out clear. Webb the spider clenched his jointed legs on P.H.'s back. Webb spread silk from his spinneret at a nearby pole. He and P.H. went into the hole and they sank slowly down to the three heroes. P.H. had the key in his beak. Slippy the slug grabbed onto the silk string with his slimy foot and slid down to Webb and P.H.

"Look out below!" he said. Then he fell down on P.H. next to Webb and grabbed the key from P.H.'s mouth holding it with his anterior tentacles.

"Okay, P.H., open your mouth!" Whip commanded. "I'm going to shoot my tongue."

"Why should I open my mouth for *that?*" asked P.H.

"Just do it, quick!" said Slippy.

"Go like 'Awwwwk!" Bobi showed the trick with his jaws widened.

"Okay," said P.H. He opened his beak. "Auuughhh!"

Whip shot his tongue out of his mouth into P.H.'s open beak. P.H. caught it in between his mandibles. Slippy slid onto his beak then to Whip's tongue.

"I'm going aboard," he said.

"O'gay, B-eighth," Whip said with his tongue still out. "Yuh kin led go now."

"RR?" P.H. squawked with Whip's tongue in his mouth.

"You can let go now, P.H.," said Pition.

So P.H. released Whip's tongue which shot back to his mouth with Slippy.

"Mph!" said Slippy as he got slammed at Whip's mouth. "Don't bother tasting my slime." He climbed up Whip's face. Then he slid on his arm to reach the shackle on his wrist. Slippy unlocked it with the key. Whip moved his arm with Slippy to his other arm, so Slippy could unlock the other shackle. Whip finally landed to the floor. Slippy tossed the key back up to P.H., so he could free the others. He unlocked the shackle with Pition's neck. Pition's head fell low to the wall's lower section.

"Whoa," he said.

P.H. unlocked the shackle with Pition's tail. Pition fell to the floor.

"Oof," he said.

P.H. flew to Bobi. As P.H. unlocked the shackles, Bobi complained, "Hey, watch it. Ow! WHOA!" He fell to the floor after P.H. unlocked the shackles.

"Ow!" Bobi cried.

Whip walked toward a nearby window and witnessed the Satvrinskis' palace and the small town in front of it. A mumbling sound occurred.

"What the--?" Whip said as he heard it. "Pition!"

It was Pition with the frog that fell in the cell, in his mouth. He spat him out.

"Sorry about that," Pition said.

"Quit nagging around," said Whip, "we've gotta stop that sacrifice and save my sister!"

Bobi lifted himself up and said, "I thought you were just gonna let those tigers babysit your sister."

"I was, but I can't let them do this to her," said Whip.

"BOOM! Shacka lacka!" Bobi shouted. "That's what I like to hear! Look who's finally coming back!"

"But this is impossible," said Pition. "We'll never make it there; it'll be crawling with soldiers."

"Let's go!" Whip commanded.

So our heroes and the animals walked out of the prison. They dashed and slid down the snowy slope next to it. There were no guards by the doors, because the prison was old. As they all ended up at the bottom of the slope, there lay a mound of snow.

"This is where we parked the World Bug," said Kirbo the cassowary.

Whip wiped some snow away and he could recognize his invented vehicle.

"Thanks, guys," he said.

Slippy jumped off of Whip's arm and slid up the snowy cover on the World Bug.

"Well, guys, it looks like we're getting squashed into a pile of dead tomato frogs," he said. He set his tentacles over the snow. Whip smiled at Slippy. Slippy looked up at him and said, "What?"

"Have you ever been to a sushi restaurant?" Whip asked him.

"Why, yes. They serve all kinds of dead tropical fish and stuff," said Slippy. "Why do you ask?"

"Because we're gonna need calamari," said Whip, "lots and lots of calamari."

CHAPTER 21

Squid Time

And so, Whip and the crew entered the Siberian town. Whip suddenly found a sushi restaurant on a nearby street. He, with Slippy the slug on his jacket's sleeve, went to the front door of that restaurant. He knocked on the door. The chef answered it. He was an old man with a large gray moustache.

"Customers?" he said.

"Hello, do you have a giant squid in your kitchen that we can use?" asked Slippy.

"Well, I do have…one," said the chef. He ran into the kitchen and grabbed a large tank with a red-orange giant squid. He pushed the tank on a rolling cart to the front door. The squid was sleeping. Whip woke it up with his psychic powers. The squid woke up and grew angry. The chef dashed back in the restaurant. The squid grew large and broke its tank. Water spewed everywhere. The chef warned the people of the uprising squid.

"Duck and cover!" he shouted.

"It's ALIVE!" yelled Slippy.

Whip got up on the squid's head for the ride. Suddenly, the squid caused a rampage over the town. People screamed in horror. The squid slammed one tentacle, causing a quake on the next street. It howled and groaned.

"Go, Gigo, go!" Whip shouted as the squid advanced. Gigo was the squid's given name.

Pition and most of the animals rode on Bobi's back as Bobi flew. Kirbo and Sampson were moving along the road. Whip found the Satvrinskis' palace.

"There it is, Gigo," he said to the squid, "to the palace."

The squid grabbed a giant wood-carved fish from the top of a nearby market.

"No, no!" shouted Whip. "We're not going for that! Put that down!"

The squid dropped the fish. Bobi flew down to the squid.

"Hey, Gigo, over here!" he called. "Look at the dragon!"

The squid moaned.

"That's right, follow the dragon!" said Bobi. "He'll lead you to your destiny."

The squid slowly followed Bobi as he flew.

"Hey, Bobi!" Whip called to him. "Make sure you fly slowly, 'cause this beast doesn't move fast enough on land!"

"Alright!" Bobi said as he heard Whip.

CHAPTER 22

The Sacrifice Is About to Begin

The ceremony was being run. People were dancing; Abmora was leading the music; and Aborabor took Sarah down the stairs to the courtyard out back. Sarah was dressed in a bright pink dress with a golden belt. Aborabor kissed his paw, waving it to the crowd.

"What on Earth are you doing?" Sarah asked him.

"Oh, I'm just...playing my part," said Aborabor.

"Are you wearing lipstick?" Sarah asked as she witnessed Aborabor's lips being purple.

"Uh...actually it's lip *gloss,*" said Aborabor. "It's a grape flavor. Would you like a taste?"

"Ugh! You act even weirder than my brother!" Sarah ran some steps back up.

"Oh, nonsense," Aborabor chuckled as he went back up to get Sarah.

Abmora was presenting a pit surrounded by tiles of the backyard. The pit had green mist escaping it. Above it was a cage held by a hook on a chain activated by a pulley. A pianist was playing the music for the ceremony.

"Now, let us have some opera music!" Abmora commanded in a microphone.

So the pianist continued. Musicians raised their wind and string instruments. They all played an orchestra for the ceremony. As Aborabor reached his paw to Sarah, he said, "Here, don't be afraid. Follow me. It'll be harmless."

Sarah followed him down the stairs to the pit of green mist. Abmora led the music on a bandstand.

As the music grew louder, Whip and the crew outside the front of the palace, led the squid to break off the tall front doors.

"Alright, big fella!" said Whip. "Let's smash this palace apart."

The squid approached the palace. Suddenly, a roof guard gave a warning in Russian. He commanded the other guards to ready a catapult to fire a burning ball. As they did, Whip's friends panicked.

"Brace yourselves!" shouted Whip.

As the squid looked at the fireball, it raised one of its tentacles and whacked the ball back to the guards. The fireball hit and the destroyed the catapult.

"WHOA, MAYBE!" Bobi shouted out.

Back in the courtyard, Abmora pulled and tugged on the chain of the pulley to lower the cage over the pit, so that Aborabor would make sure that Sarah was ready. Outside the front of the palace the squid approached the doors.

"After you, Gigo," said Whip.

The squid used its tentacles to break through windows and pull on the doors to open them. The guards called a helicopter. The helicopter flew from far away and hovered above the squid. The pilot dropped a bomb and the squid lifted a tentacle to whack the bomb away. It exploded at a faraway hill. The squid grabbed a nearby tree and threw it up at the helicopter. The helicopter blew up into spare parts as the pilot jumped out with a parachute. And so, the squid continued to push the doors out toward itself from the inside. As the door fell free, other guards brought a mortar cannon. They shot a mortar at the squid. The squid fell backward a bit. Whip carefully held onto the squid's top to avoid falling.

"WHIP!" Bobi shouted.

The squid was still up and ready to rip. Whip looked and witnessed a place to sneak. The guards shot another mortar at the squid. Whip jumped down to the snow, and Slippy slid off his arm and fell down to the falling wounded squid that fell to the snow. Whip dashed to the side of the palace.

Back in the courtyard, Aborabor put Sarah in the cage over the green pit. Sarah shook and shivered in panic.

"Don't worry," said Aborabor. "Everything will be perfectly fine as you go down there."

As our heroes waited outside, Whip snuck into a window and climbed through it from the side. He tapped a guard's shoulder and gave him a punch at his face. Whip jumped on the cannon and performed a break dance, attacking the guards with Kung Fu kicks. As they fell, the cannon fell on the floor. Whip whistled to his pals.

"Come on!" he shouted, waving his arm up over his head. The crew cheered, except for Slippy, whining to the dying squid. The squid groaned until it finally died. Slippy cried. Pango the pangolin grabbed Slippy with his worm like tongue and tossed him toward the others. Slippy flew through midair. Sampson the seal caught him in his mouth. Pition rode Bobi, who ran to Whip. He jumped on Bobi's back. The three heroes went through the palace hallway. A group of guards suddenly blocked their path.

"Whoa," said Whip.

Bobi jumped over the guards. He spread his wings to glide to the other side. Then he landed. He continued running to the back of the palace as the guards chased after the heroes. Suddenly, Pition had an idea. He jumped off of Bobi and landed between a pair of doors.

"Pition!" Whip shouted. He braked Bobi for a second.

"Go ahead without me, guys!" Pition called back. "I'm taking care of these guards. Go ahead and save your sister, Whip!"

So Whip and Bobi went ahead. Pition made a slight expression of sadness as he lay on the floor. As the guards approached him, they stopped and stared at him with thoughts of a lonely snake.

"Awwwe," the guards bellowed.

Pition suddenly awoke and struck upon the guards. He bit them with poisonous punctures and whacked their helmets with his tail. He suddenly killed them after a moment of attack.

CHAPTER 23

Whip to the Rescue

As Whip and Bobi dashed to the back doors, Abmora tugged on the pulley chain about to lower the cage with Sarah in the pit. All of a sudden, Whip and Bobi finally crashed the doors open.

"STOP!" Whip shouted.

The audience gasped. Aborabor turned and witnessed them. Sarah found her brother in surprise. Abmora growled raising her fist in front of her head.

"Look out! Dragon coming through!" said Bobi as he ran down the stairs between two audience aisles.

"Hey, Chester Cheetah!" Whip called to Aborabor. He jumped off of Bobi's back and walked towards Aborabor, pointing and frowning at him. "Back away from my sister."

"Whip!" Sarah said in shock.

Abmora grabbed her scepter and walked toward Whip saying, "You can just go back to your home and leave well enough alone by waiting for your family there."

"ANIMALS, ATTACK!" Whip shouted for the animals coming to the courtyard from the sides of the palace.

Webb the spider had spun a web used for a trampoline. He, Pango, and Sampson brought it on a rolling board.

"Web tramp!" they shouted. Sampson jumped on the tramp and leaped high into the air.

"To infinity and beyond!" he shouted as he aimed for Abmora. He landed on her back and bounced on her.

"P.H!" Whip called for that parrot. "Get the scepter!"

P.H. flew for Abmora's scepter, squawking and saying, "Get the scepter! Get the scepter!" But as he almost touched it, Abmora shot a beam from it that turned P.H. into a chicken. P.H. squawked and gobbled. Abmora grabbed Sampson by the tail and spun and tossed him to the audience.

"I'm alright," said Sampson as he landed on an aisle seat.

Abmora raised her scepter about to zap Whip, but Kirbo the cassowary quickly bit her on her arm. Abmora accidentally tossed her scepter backwards. Kirbo let go of her. As the scepter flew in midair, Pango the pangolin leaped up and caught it. He rolled into a ball as he held the scepter. As he landed on the tile floor, he tossed the scepter to Bobi. He caught it in his mouth then he flew up in the air.

"Come back down with that this instant!" yelled Abmora.

As Bobi flew around more, he dropped the scepter back to the floor. Slippy went by as the scepter landed on its bottom end. Slippy rolled like a barrel away from it.

"I nearly panicked there," he said as he slid away.

The four fat frogs caught the scepter. They zapped it to turn P.H. back into his parrot self.

"BWARK!" P.H. squawked. "I'm back!"

The four fat frogs used the scepter for bait.

"Looking for this, madam?" they asked Abmora from a few yards away. Abmora ran to it then so did Whip.

"That's mine. That's mine," Abmora said as she got to where her scepter was. As she picked it up, Whip knocked it out of her paws. The scepter flew near the back porch of the palace. Pition appeared in the doorway. He slid and jumped fast down the stairs. Bobi ran under the scepter's flight. Pition leaped up and caught the scepter in his coiling body's grasp. Bobi halted and Pition landed on his back.

"Pray for mercy from a dragon..." said Bobi.

"...and a strange snake," said Pition.

Abmora came about the cage with Sarah.

"She's taken the potion!" she shouted to her son. "Drop her in the pit, now!" That was her command. Aborabor pushed the cage with Sarah down into the misty, green pit.

CHAPTER 24

It's Too Late

"**N**O!" shouted Whip.

Bobi slapped his face. Pition hissed in panic. Whip's parents appeared doubtful. The Satvrinskis' plan was finally coming together. As Sarah sank in the pit with green mist everywhere, three purple spirits were flying in a circle. As Sarah landed on a solid platform, one of the spirits faced her, asking, "Do you wish to accept knowledge for the real world?"

"Yes," said Sarah as she gulped feeling shy. The spirit backed up and zoomed into her body. It swam around to make Sarah's mind right and ready for a good education in school. Then the spirit went out when it was done. Sarah hovered and floated back to the overworld.

CHAPTER 25

But Wait!

As she got back up, she faced Aborabor. Aborabor looked down. Suddenly, Sarah lifted her foot and kicked Aborabor in his chin. Sarah's body flipped and she landed back on her feet.

"Ohhhh!" bellowed the audience.

"Oh-uhhhh..." Aborabor bellowed as he fainted. Sarah ran to her brother.

"Whip," she said.

"Sorry, Sarah," Whip said to her. So the Psy family was reunited.

"Tehran!" Abmora shouted. She went to Tehran and said, "You were supposed to give her that potion!" She pointed at him as she scolded.

"Well," said Tehran. "I guess I gave her the wrong cup of chocolate." He walked forward as he confronted Abmora.

"Mother!" Aborabor shouted as he got up and grabbed the scepter from Pition. Pition fell off as he let go. Aborabor tossed the scepter back to his mother. Abmora caught it.

"RRGH!" she growled. "I once told you, Whip, that I didn't need assistance. By the way, your myth has never been DISCOVERED!!" She zapped a beam from her scepter at Whip and Sarah. Tehran quickly ran by his children and formed a giant force shield around them that fended off the scepter's beam. It was reflected up to the night sky. Bobi spewed a fireball from his mouth at it. Tehran kept the force shield up. Abmora was getting angrier. Suddenly, a shot from a machine gun knocked away her scepter. It was Fentruck Tusker.

CHAPTER 26

Fentruck Saves the Day

"FENTRUCK!" Whip shouted as he witnessed Fentruck.
Fentruck sprung into action with his new machine gun.
"Surprise, surprise," he said.

Abmora reached for her scepter and it hovered and shot straight back to her paw with magic. Fentruck used his machine gun in combat using it to battle as a rod-like weapon against Abmora, who used her scepter. The animals rejoined each other and grouped together to watch the battle go on. Suddenly, Abmora wound up a round beam at the top of her scepter which knocked away Fentruck's machine gun. Fentruck ran away from the fight. As Abmora tried to create madness with the Psy family, Tehran blocked her scepter when she was about to cast a spell on them.

"So, Tehran," she said. "What are you going to do about this?"

"This is for my son!" Tehran shouted and stomped Abmora's hind paw. "This one's for my daughter!" He punched her. Abmora fell backward on the ground as Tehran held the scepter raising it and turning it upside down. "And this one's for you," he said, "who ruined our vacation AND our family!" He slammed the lamp-like top end of the scepter, in which the glass cracked spreading purple lightning that electrocuted Abmora. Abmora shook as she was shocked. Suddenly, the glass of the scepter's head broke away and exploded like a purple bomb. Abmora turned into her skeleton. She fell apart on the ground. And Tsarina Abmora Satvrinski was defeated.

CHAPTER 27

The End of a Bizarre Vacation

Some of the lightning shocked Tehran. He fell forward and lay asleep in a faint.

"Dad," said Whip. The Psy family went to Tehran. They carefully leaned over him without falling.

"Is he…?" asked Sampson the seal.

"Yep," said Slippy the slug, quite grieving. Suddenly, the purple spirits from the green pit flew to Tehran to revive him.

"Whoa, spirits!" said Slippy in shock. The spirits went into Tehran's body to lift him up as he still seemed asleep. Then he woke up.

"Tehran!" Corbin said in surprise to see her husband awake.

"Dad!" Whip and Sarah both said simultaneously in surprise as well.

"I hoped you would never see me do that," Tehran said. "I had to drink the potion to get used to wisdom, only to save our family from that white tigress." He pointed to Abmora's skeleton on the floor.

"I guess your daughter gave you hard times," said Bobi. "Maybe you shouldn't have her at all."

"Bobi!" Whip scolded.

"No, no, he's right, forgive me," said Tehran. He got his next idea. "Whip, would you make sure that Sarah doesn't mess around and does her homework. I'm afraid I have to leave." He started to walk away.

"Tehran," said Corbin nearly disappointed.

"I'm sorry, Corbin," said Tehran. "I just wish I could be man you once deserved." Corbin touched her husband's shoulder.

"But you are that man," she said, "...just like always." Tehran nearly closed his eyes.

"I guess Tehran really knew how to fight a woman here," said Bobi, looking at Abmora's skeleton.

Suddenly, the clock above the back doors struck to midnight. Its bells rang.

"WHIP!" Pition called out. "The 'Eternal Life' potion!"

"Midnight!" said Whip. "Right." He turned to his sister and said, "Sarah, I can promise you everything that I can be nice to you, no matter what happens."

"Huh?" Sarah wondered.

"I mean..." Whip continued. "If you would do better in school and if I would compromise, we can all live forever."

"Really?" Sarah asked.

"Yes," said Whip. Sarah looked around gathering thoughts.

"I would deserve any treat for doing any good in school," she said, "maybe ice cream or something."

"That's good," said Whip. And he smiled, then so did Sarah.

"Whatever happens," said Pition shivering in panic, "I shouldn't cry." He set his eyes on his tail.

Suddenly, Whip started to hover above the ground, then so did Bobi and Pition. Whip shone a golden light that was as bright as any bright star. The audience covered their eyes. The animals awed at the sight. Bobi and Pition were turning back to their real selves.

"Huh, oh no!" said Bobi witnessing his dragon hands turning back into crocodile ones. His horns and ears disappeared. His tail shrunk back to his thick, scaly crocodile tail. Then his wings disappeared. "Oh no," he whimpered.

Pition's new coloring turned all black. The horn on his muzzle and the blade on his tail disappeared. And so, Whip, Bobi, and Pition were back to normal. They landed back on solid ground. Whip laughed and turned to Bobi and said, "Hey, you still look like a vicious monster to me."

Bobi smiled, then so did Pition. The people in the audience clapped their hands repeatedly.

Suddenly, Tehran had an announcement to make. He raised his arms and shouted, "Ladies and gentlemen!" Then he lowered his arms and continued, "This vacation was all a mistake. I meant to go to Canada, but these white tigers made me bring my daughter to this sacrificial plan. So I believe whoever saved us was this walrus, Fentruck Tusker."

When Fentruck heard his name, he grabbed his machine gun and joined together with the Psy family.

"I was honored," said Fentruck.

"How would you like to live with us?" asked Whip.

"I'd be delighted," said Fentruck. "I haven't had a home for many years since I've traveled. I'd be honored to be your roommate." So Fentruck became a new member of the Whip team.

Suddenly, Crow Buck flew to them saying to Fentruck, "Congratulations, Fenny. You're getting a new home."

"Indeed I am," said Fentruck. So they all lived happily ever after... for now.

EPILOGUE

The Psyvark Always Comes in Peace

Because of the mythical and ingenious adventures of Whip, he has become famous for his intelligence. He and his friends first fought the evil Vips at the store during the night after Whip's family visited Tehran's brother and father. And at this recent time, they stopped some evil white tigers from pulverizing Sarah's lonely and shy mind. A psyvark had to do what a psyvark had to do.

THE END

Other books by Tyler Johns:

The Sharp Empire
The Sharp Empire II: The Serpent Strikes Back
The Sharp Empire III: The Phantom of the Galaxy
The Sharp Empire IV: Return of the Gospel
Whip

Coming Soon:
Whip 3: Whip's Extreme Adventure